Pete, 'World's Oldest Pigeon,' Vanishes Again; Police, Children Hunt for Feathered Friend

The oldest pigeon in the world—according to his worried owner—is lost. He is Pete, 14 years old, who lives with Jesse J. Jones, Baltimore & Ohio Railroad engineer, in the first block E. Ostend St. He went for his usual constitutional stroll yesterday and has not been seen since.

Mr. Jones has offered a reward of $5, and all of Pete's friends in South Baltimore, including hundreds of children and the staff of the Southern Police Station, are hunting for him.

Pete can be recognized by a daub of red paint on his head, by his unconquerable fear of umbrellas and by his liking for milk and coffee—provided it is offered in an aluminum cup.

A Really Remarkable Bird

The finder of Pete will have in his possession, for awhile, the oldest pigeon in the world, according to Mr. Jones.

Pigeons ordinarily live to be 8 or 10 years old. The agricultural department in Washington has authentic proof of a few pigeons which have lived 12 years. Pete is 14 years old, according to Mr. Jones.

It was in the spring of 1919 when Mr. Jones' father, a painter, found Pete, a featherless squab, in a nest uptown. He put the naked little bird in his pocket, took it home, and there it has remained ever since—except for two other occasions when Pete was stolen.

Once a plumber took a fancy to Pete, Mr. Jones said, and walked off with him. Another time a Negro found Pete out for a stroll. Mr. Jones rescued him just as the hatchet was about to descend on his head.

"Pete was feeling fine this morning," Mr. Jones said. "He had taken his morning nip of milk and coffee, which he will drink only if offered in his own aluminum cup. Then he had gone out for his morning constitutional.

"I am sure he was not run over. He rarely flies, as he loves the exercise of walking. But he observes traffic regulations religiously, standing on the curb and cooing for a lift across the street when traffic is heavy.

"He has been a frequent visitor to the Southern Police Station, loving to perch on the brass rail of the desk and see that things are run right. The police and all the neighbors know him."

The daub of red paint on Pete's head was obtained when Pete decided to inspect a paint brush Monday when Mr. Jones was doing an off-day job at home.

"About the only bad habit Pete has is pulling out electric plugs and pulling new brooms to pieces to make nests in my shoes," Mr. Jones said. "He perches on the back of my chair when I read the evening paper and he hops upon the radio and calls for someone to turn it on when he wants music."

Pete is fond of children, but keeps a wise weather eye open for all cats, which he has been dodging for all 14 years of his life.

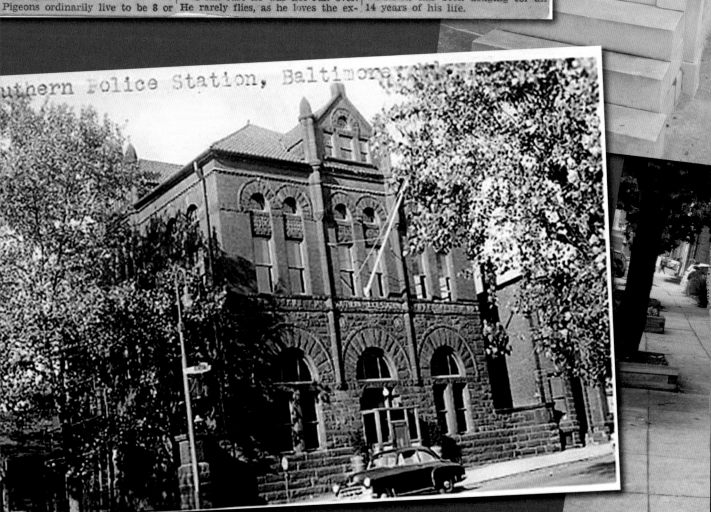

Southern Police Station, Baltimore

Pigeon Methuselah Comes Home

Venerable Blue Pigeon Back Again In Cage

And He Has Been There Since 7.30 Wednesday Afternoon When Boy Returned Him

The kidnapping theory of Pete, South Baltimore's aged blue pigeon, has blown up completely.

It was reported yesterday that the 14-year-old bird was missing from his home in the first block Ostend street and that kidnapping was feared. As a matter of fact Pete was home and had been since 7.30 P. M. Wednesday when he was returned by a small boy, whose name was not revealed.

The pigeon, the property of Jesse Jones, disappeared Wednesday morning. He was out in front of his home and a boy, not knowing where the bird lived, picked him up and carried him away. A few hours later he was released and the second boy took possession of him, but only for a few hours, and then returned him to the Joneses.

Miss Muriel Jones and Pete

Pete, the Methuselah among pigeons at his hoary age of 14 years, is shown here with Miss Jones after his return to the Jones homestead in the first block E. Ostend St. after an unauthorized absence of one day. Pete was reported missing yesterday, and a $5 reward by his owner, Jesse J. Jones, led to his return last night. The average age of a pigeon, it is said, is less than 10 years, but Pete has far outlived his contemporaries.

Dear Reader,

This is the true story about my remarkable life as an ordinary street pigeon. The events and activities in this book were taken from several local newspaper articles written about me during my lifetime. This story faithfully recreates much of my life as a tribute to my person, Muriel. I hope you enjoy reading about it as much as I enjoyed living it with her!

Sincerely,

Pete

Special Thanks...

I would like to thank the children of Muriel, Gary Meyers and Eileen (Meyers) Donnelly, for making this book possible and allowing me to share my remarkable life's story with others. Although I never met Gary, I actually lived and played with Eileen during the first couple years of her life. I remember her picking me up by my neck and hugging me. Eileen provided all of the information used in my book. Gary organized the written material into a storyline with their spouses, John and Darlene, helping with the wording. Thanks also to their friends Sharon, Candy, and Jan for offering suggestions throughout the publishing process. A special thanks to editors Meghan Reynolds and Laura Carroll who took our original script and made it look professional. And finally, a heartfelt thanks to my illustrator Stephanie Helgeson who brought all of these words to life.

www.mascotbooks.com

The Autobiography of A Pigeon Named Pete: A True Baltimore Story

For more information, please contact:
Mascot Books
560 Herndon Parkway #120
Herndon, VA 20170
info@mascotbooks.com

Library of Congress Control Number: 2016910063

CPSIA Code: PRT0916A
ISBN: 978-1-63177-269-6

Printed in the United States

The Autobiography of
A Pigeon Named Pete

Hope you enjoy!

Gary Meyers

A True Baltimore Story

By Pete the Pigeon   **Interpreted by Gary Meyers**

Illustrated by Stephanie Helgeson

I was born with my sister and brother in an ordinary pigeon nest on the roof of a tall city building. Although my mother and father tried to feed us all, I never got enough to eat. One day an ordinary painter working near my nest saw that I was hungry, so he picked me up and put me in his pocket to take to his granddaughter, Muriel.

Muriel lived with her family in an ordinary row house on an ordinary street. I was given my own birdcage with food and fresh water. Soon after, I was given a name by the family: Pete.

No other pigeon in Baltimore had any of these things, especially their own person!

I was truly EXTRAORDINARY!

Muriel was very young...about as old as I was in pigeon years!
Over many years, Muriel and I grew up together, played
together, and loved each other more and more every day.
Muriel talked to me kindly and loved to pet me. I loved to be
petted, though eating was still my favorite thing.

I always wanted to be with Muriel and I slept beside her bed in my cage every night. As I grew and became stronger, I needed freedom. After all, I was an outdoor bird, and Muriel knew that!

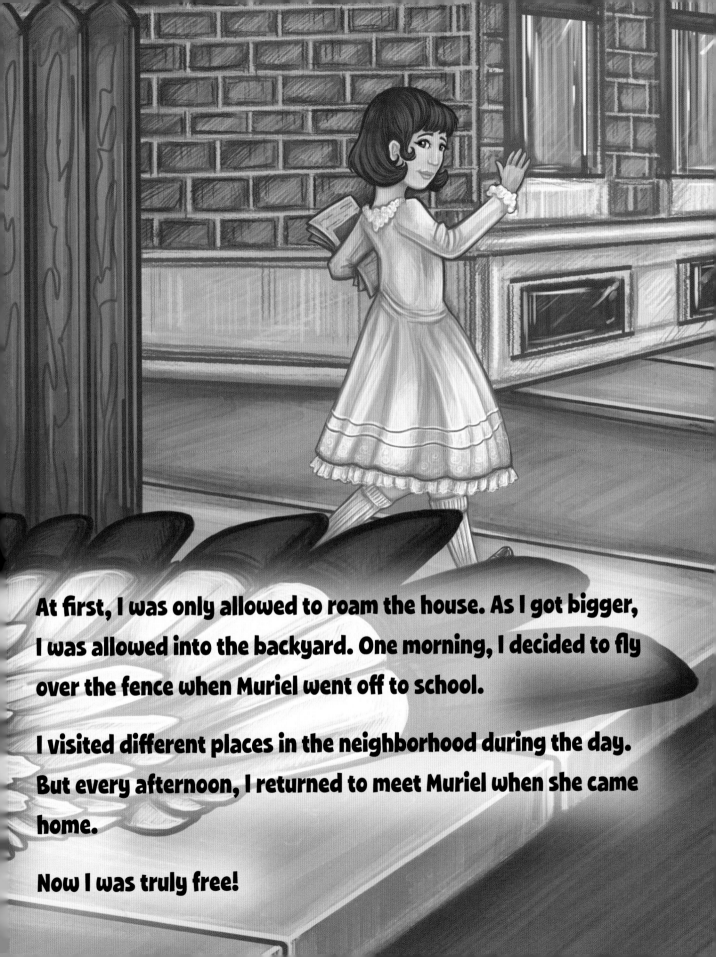

At first, I was only allowed to roam the house. As I got bigger, I was allowed into the backyard. One morning, I decided to fly over the fence when Muriel went off to school.

I visited different places in the neighborhood during the day. But every afternoon, I returned to meet Muriel when she came home.

Now I was truly free!

Every morning while Muriel had breakfast, I had a sip of milk and coffee from my own cup. During the day while she was away, I visited my favorite places.

I walked the sidewalks of Baltimore until someone picked me up and petted me. Some even helped me cross the street if there was too much traffic. It was just too slow and dangerous to do it on my pigeon feet. I made lots of friends.

I flew to many neighboring kitchen windowsills for tasty treats. The neighbors loved my company and were more than happy to feed and pet me.

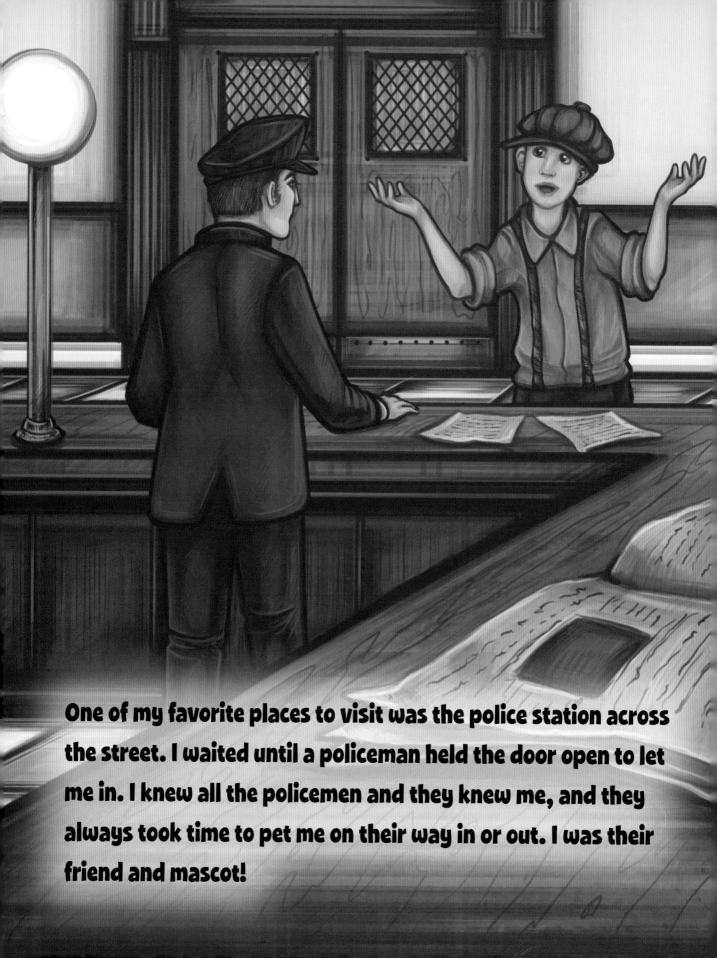

One of my favorite places to visit was the police station across the street. I waited until a policeman held the door open to let me in. I knew all the policemen and they knew me, and they always took time to pet me on their way in or out. I was their friend and mascot!

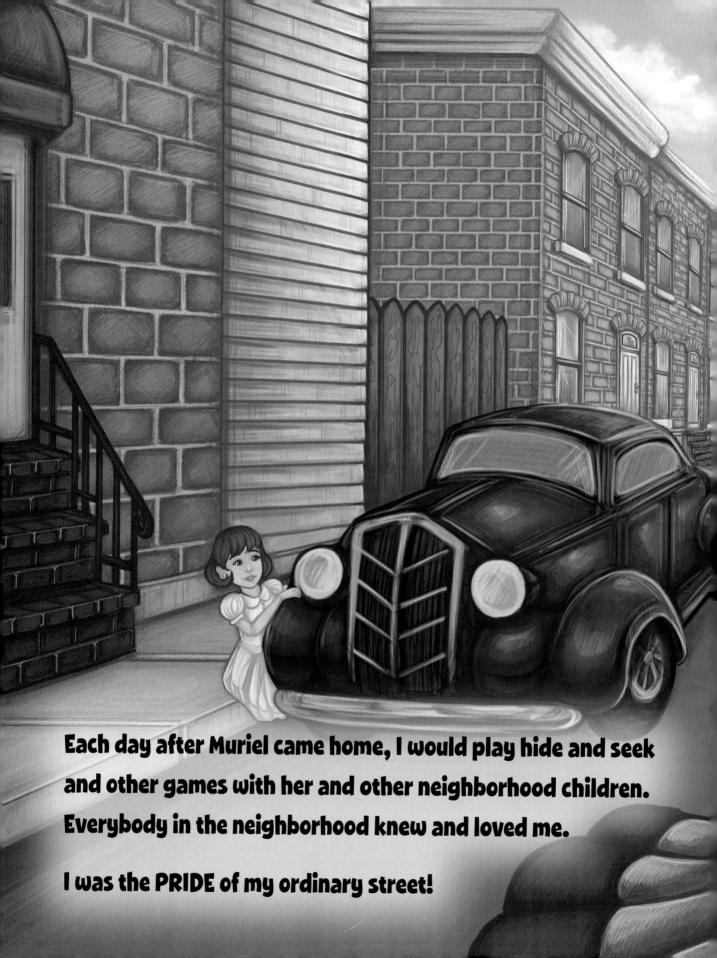

Each day after Muriel came home, I would play hide and seek and other games with her and other neighborhood children. Everybody in the neighborhood knew and loved me.

I was the PRIDE of my ordinary street!

I was a character. I had a bad habit of pulling bristles from new straw brooms, biting them to pieces, and making nests in the shoes of Muriel's father. I even played practical jokes on her mother by pulling the plug of the iron while she was ironing.

Every evening, I sat on the back of the big lounge chair while Father read the newspaper.

If I got bored, I hopped onto the radio and cooed until someone turned it on. I was also a great "watch pigeon," fluttering my feathers and wings when any stranger came around.

One day when Muriel came home, I wasn't there. She waited and called for me but I did not show up. Hundreds of policemen and neighbors including children, searched for me. Muriel's father even offered a reward for my safe return.

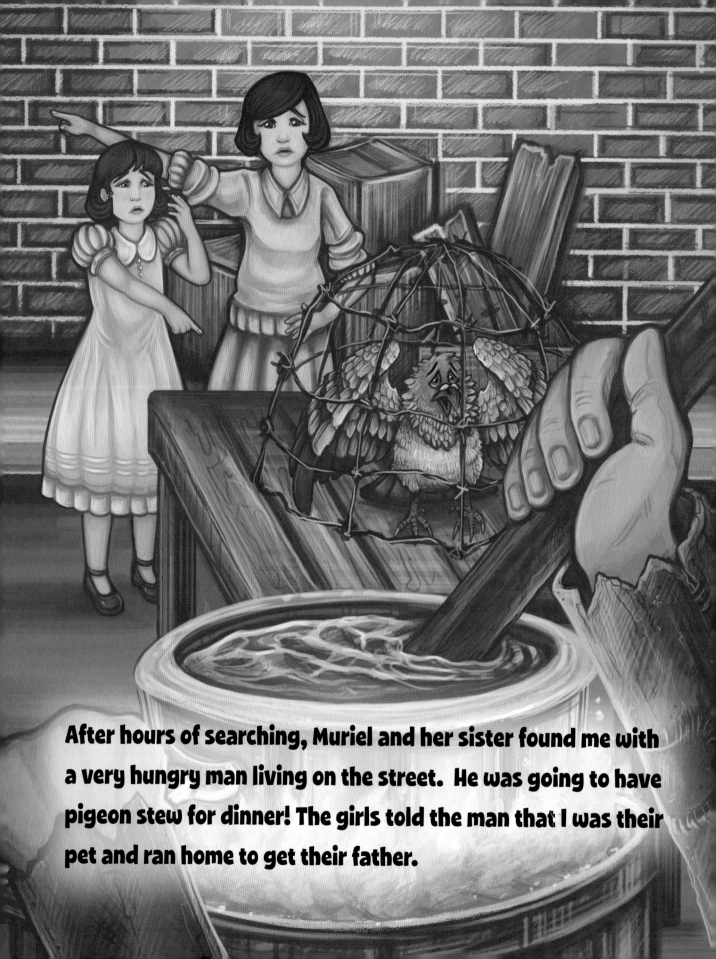

After hours of searching, Muriel and her sister found me with a very hungry man living on the street. He was going to have pigeon stew for dinner! The girls told the man that I was their pet and ran home to get their father.

He went back with them and gave the man some money to buy plenty of food. The man was happy to get money and happy to let me go home with my loving family.

Not only was I EXTRAORDINARY...I was one LUCKY pigeon!

I had quite the adventurous life and lived to be twenty-five years old, over twice as long as ordinary street pigeons. I was buried in a special place along with other extraordinary pets.

If you ever find yourself near Baltimore and would like to see the row house where I lived, or if you would like to see the special place where I now rest, just turn the page...

In loving memory of Pete

and his person...Muriel

Horsefeathers and Pete! 2/6

—American Staff Photo.

MURIEL JONES, nine, 19 East Ostend street, and others in her family say folks think they are giving them a lot of Barney Google's horsefeathers when they tell of the things their pet pigeon Pete can do. His feathers, whatever they are, show sheer intelligence and can make you laugh, too. Besides being a real pet he is also a good watcher, for he flits and flutters about to attract attention of the family when strangers come near.

THE ROSA BONHEUR MEMORIAL, Inc.

A Modern Pet Animal Cemetery Under Perpetual Care

WASHINGTON BLVD. at DORSEY ROAD
ELKRIDGE, MARYLAND

BALTIMORE CITY OFFICE
1201 W. FAYETTE STREET

PHONE:
ELkRIDGE 348

THIS AGREEMENT, made and entered into this ___12-th___ day of ___May___ 19_44_ by and between The Rosa Bonheur Memorial, Inc., a Maryland Corporation, of Baltimore, Md., designated "SELLER" and ___Jesse Jones,___ of ___19 E.Ostend.St Balto.Md.___ designated "PURCHASER"

WITNESSETH: That Purchaser hereby purchases from Seller the perpetual and exclusive use forever of the following:

One Quarter ___-1/4___ One Half XXXXXXXXXXXXX Full Lot No. ___#1-___

Section ___-Queen,___ Block ___Front Point___ Grave ___--A--___

___Complete Interment, Concrete Marker. (R3bate on Bronze)___

___The Rosa Bonheur Memorial a burial ground for pets and animals situated on the Washington Boulevard, Howard County, Maryland, and agrees to pay therefor the sum of ___Ten--------------------___ Dollars ($___10.00___)

as follows: in cash, ___Seven--------___ Down Payment ($___7.00___) the receipt of which is hereby acknowledged.

PET SPEC. ___Pidgeon.___

NAME ___-*PETE*-___

___1919--1944___

Balance due ($___3.00___)

ROSA BONHEUR MEMORIAL, INC.

per_____

This Deed. Made this 27th day of May, in the year 1944, between ROSA BONHEUR MEMORIAL, INC. (Pet Animal Cemetery) a body corporate of the State of Maryland, hereinafter called the Company, which term shall include the successors and assigns of said Company, and Mrs. Jesse Jones, 19 E. Ostend Street, Baltimore, Maryland.

hereinafter called Purchaser, which term shall include the plural as well as the singular and the heirs and assigns of said party or parties.

WITNESSETH: That in consideration of the payment of One ($1.00) and No/100 Dollars and other good and valuable considerations, the Company doth grant, assign and convey unto the Purchaser, subject to the restrictions hereinafter referred to and for the purposes of burial only, the use of

1/4 Lot No. 1 Size 2' X 4' Single Grave No. A Block No. Front Point Sec. Queen

in the Cemetery or Memorial Park of the Company, situate in Howard County, State of Maryland, as shown on the plat of said Cemetery or Memorial Park on file at the office of the Company.

TO HAVE AND TO HOLD the use of the herein described lot or single grave unto the Purchaser, forever, for burial purposes only, subject to such conditions, restrictions, rules, and/or regulations as are now or may hereafter be imposed by the Company for the care, maintenance, control and use of the Cemetery or Memorial Park property. The Purchaser agrees that the use or occupation of above described lot or single grave will always be in conformity with the aforesaid conditions, restrictions, rules and/or regulations, and will, upon the request of the Company change, modify or correct any use made thereof not in conformity with the said conditions, restrictions, rules and/or regulations, which are on file in the office of the Company.

In testimony whereof, the Company has caused its name to be hereto signed by Edward Gross its (Vice) President and its Corporate Seal to be hereunto affixed and attested by its (Asst.) Secretary.

TEST:

ROSA BONHEUR MEMORIAL, INC.

_____ SECRETARY.

Edward Gross PRESIDENT.

Pete's home on the corner of Ostend and Patapsco Streets

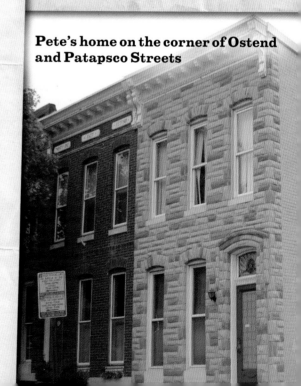

Rosa Bonheur Memorial, Inc.

A Modern and Beautiful Burial Park for Pet Animals
Under Perpetual Care

BURIAL PARK
Washington Blvd. at Dorsey Lane
Howard County, Md.
Phone, Elkridge 348

BALTIMORE OFFICE
1201 W. Fayette Street
Baltimore, Md.
Phone, Calvert 5042

June 8, 1944

Mrs. Jesse Jones,
19 E. Ostend Street,
Baltimore, Maryland.

Dear Mrs. Jones:

We are enclosing herewith your Deed to the Burial plot of your Pet, Pete, and also pictures which were taken at the time of burial.

We wish to extend our gratitude for your interest in our endeavor. Such interest is manifest and adds so much encouragement to the management who have put their faith and efforts in determining to build this desirable resting place for Pet Animals, primarily established for those of us who love their Pets and desire to give them a kindly burial.

We will be very happy indeed to have you visit the Park at any time at your convenience.

Very sincerely yours,
ROSA BONHEUR MEMORIAL, Inc.

Erna K. Tharsheim
Secretary.

EKW

Patriarch Pigeon Dead At Age Of 25

Pete is gone again—but this time for good.

His funeral will take place tomorrow, and he'll be buried beside a rosebush in the garden of Mrs. William Robbins, 3732 Columbus drive—far from his South Baltimore home, where he has spent the last 25 years in domestic bliss.

For Mrs. Robins was little Lorraine Jones, six, and her sister, the present Mrs. John Meyers, was rosy-cheeked Muriel Jones, aged eighteen months, when Pete, a foundling blue pigeon, came to their home at 19 East Ostend street.

PRIDE OF STREET

Since that day, when Lorrain and Muriel's grandfather, a painter, found Pete in a nest top one of Baltimore's tall buildings, neglected, he said, by his mother, who had other mouths to feed, Pete had become the pride of Ostend street, the playmate of the girls in hide-and-seek and other games, and the practical joker in the Jones household—he'd pull electric plugs out of their sockets while the girls' mother, Mrs. Jesse Jones, was ironing.

And during that time he was missing once, for a week; again, for several days, and once nearly became the chief ingredient in a pigeon stew when he was taken home by a passerby. Muriel and Lorraine, like the missionary in fables, came to rescue Pete from the boiling pot in the nick of time.

Pete also was a favorite of the personnel at the Southern Police Station, where he would wing several times a week to be petted.

That's all over for Pete now.

WINGS FAILED

Pete's unusual age, attested by pigeon fanciers, began to show, said his former little playmates, about five years ago, when his wings began to tire. He made fewer flights, and soon, to protect him from becoming the prey of neighborhood cats, the family kept him at home. Then his legs failed, and he was just able to get around in the Jones home.

He wasn't feeling too well last night when the family retired—and this morning they found him lifeless on the floor.

All South Baltimore will mourn Pete, especially the first block of East Ostend street—and particularly the Jones', and the Robbins', and the Meyers'.

Pete's memorial plaque is three feet from the flagpole at Rosa Bonheur Memorial Park

In Loving Memory
A Pigeon Named Pete
1919 - 1944
from His Person
Muriel (Jones) Meyers

The old South Baltimore Police Station today

Have a book idea?

Contact us at:

info@mascotbooks.com | www.mascotbooks.com